THE RAVEN'S GIFT
A TRUE STORY FROM GREENLAND

written and illustrated by **Kelly Dupre**

HOUGHTON MIFFLIN COMPANY

BOSTON 2001

With love to Lonnie—positive and persistent throughout.
Thanks for showing me how to make my dreams come true…

and for Betsy B.—a good friend, mentor, and real-life hero

All rights reserved. For information about permission to reproduce
selections from this book, write to Permissions, Houghton Mifflin Company,
215 Park Avenue South, New York, New York 10003.

www.houghtonmifflinbooks.com

The text of this book is set in 14-point Trump Mediaeval.
The illustrations are linoleum block prints with watercolor.

Library of Congress Cataloging-in-Publication Data

Dupre, Kelly.
The raven's gift: a true story from Greenland / Kelly Dupre.
p. cm.
ISBN 0-618-01171-4
1. Greenland—Description and travel—Juvenile literature. 2. Dupre, Lonnie—
Journeys—Greenland—Juvenile literature. [1. Greenland—Description and
travel. 2. Dupre, Lonnie.] I. Title.
G743.D86 2001 919.82—dc21 00-031896

Printed in Singapore
TWP 10 9 8 7 6 5 4 3 2 1

Sled Dog

Qimmiq

My name is Lonnie Dupre, and
I'm from Minnesota, U.S.A. In 1997 and
1998 John Hoelscher from Brisbane,
Australia, and I traveled by kayak and
dogsled throughout Greenland.

Greenland is a harsh but starkly beautiful
place. It is also a home to the raven. The
native people of Greenland hold the raven in
high regard. Stories about this amazing bird
go back to ancient times.

How *far does "far north" go?* I wondered as a boy. I read everything I could about the Arctic and the Inuit people who lived there.

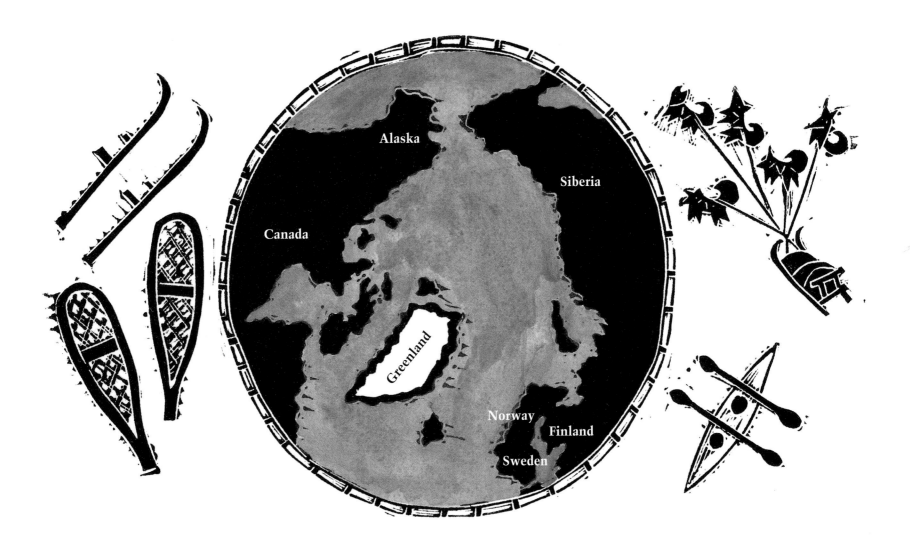

As I grew, I began to snowshoe, ski, dogsled, and kayak throughout the northern lands. I traveled to Alaska, Siberia, Canada, Norway, Finland, and Sweden. But there was one Arctic place I hadn't been to yet.

The narwhal has a ten-foot-long spiral tusk that grows out of the left side of its jaw. It is used for probing the sea bottom for food.

Polar bears live along the Arctic shores on and off the drift ice, hunting mainly seals.

Musk oxen travel in herds. One animal can weigh as much as 700 pounds. When approached, they encircle their young to protect them.

Greenland is the earth's largest island, and many unusual creatures live there.

It's also one of the homelands of the Inuit people. They have survived in the far north for thousands of years by perfecting their fascinating skills.

I have watched them make beautiful, warm fur clothing by hand and build perfectly fitted kayaks using only their arms and legs for measuring tools. During the dark polar night, they often take their dogs and sleds long distances using mainly snow ridges to help guide them.

I began to plan an expedition to Greenland. My red-haired friend John agreed to go with me. We would travel by kayak and dogsled along the Greenland coast. It took us over two years to prepare for the long journey. Our friends and family helped us plan, raise money, and pack hundreds of boxes of food and gear.

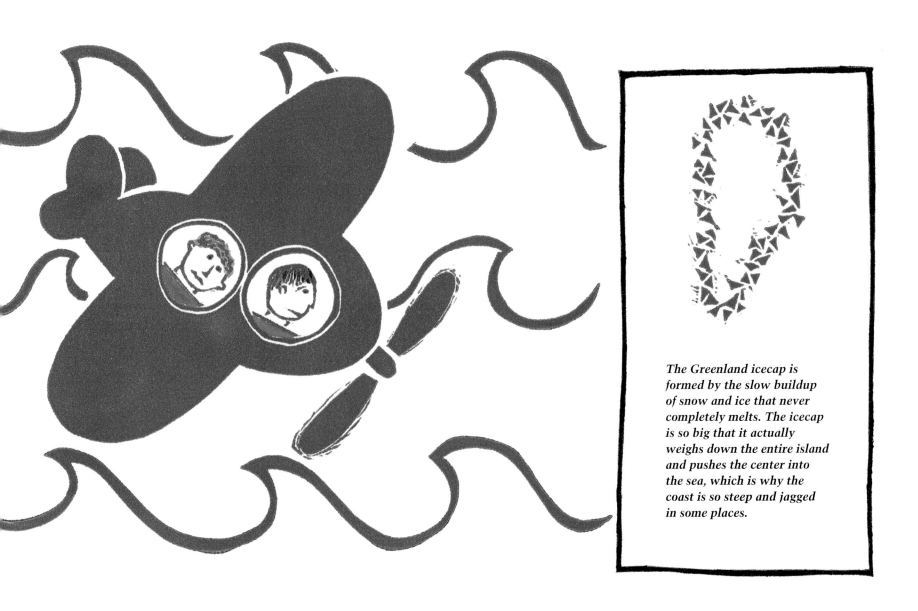

The Greenland icecap is formed by the slow buildup of snow and ice that never completely melts. The icecap is so big that it actually weighs down the entire island and pushes the center into the sea, which is why the coast is so steep and jagged in some places.

In early spring, we flew across the ocean to southwestern Greenland. As we looked down on the sharp cliffs, thick icecap, and big waves, we wondered if we were ready.

Arctic animals have evolved to survive in the harsh climate. The walrus has a thick layer of fat for warmth, can weigh up to 2,000 pounds, and lives mostly on ice floes. The caribou has hollow hairs that help keep it warm by holding in more body heat.

We began paddling north along the west coast. We saw Arctic animals like the sleek seal, strong caribou, and huge minke whale. Northern birds like the auk

Greenland is not really very green because trees can't grow there. The permafrost, or permanently frozen ground, allows for little vegetation. Erik the Red, an outlaw Viking who was exiled from both Norway and Iceland for committing several murders, was the first to call the island Greenland (Grønland). He hoped to entice others to join him there. The Inuit have their own name for their home, Kallaallit Nunaat (kay-lay-LITE noo-NA-at), "the land of the people."

and the white-tailed eagle flew around us. Tiny, colorful wildflowers grew on the rocky cliffs. We camped among giant icebergs on the treeless land.

We traveled to a different village almost every week and met many Greenlandic people. We had studied their ways to help us prepare for the expedition. From them we learned how to dress, eat, and stay warm in the cold climate. During our visits, they taught us how to predict the weather and showed us the best routes to take along the way.

Often, after an evening meal of seal, the Inuit shared with us their stories and legends. One of my favorites tells how the northern lights are the spirits of their ancestors playing ball in the sky.

Traveling was hard for the first two months. We often had stormy, windy weather. The harder we paddled, the worse things got. We felt tiny among the huge icebergs, big waves, and rocky cliffs.

Maybe we had made a mistake by coming to Greenland. We kept paddling, but each day we grew more tired. We were ready to quit.

At the end of one long day, we pulled our kayak onto the shore to make camp. As we put up the tent, we heard a strange, persistent noise coming from the high cliffs. *Aaawk! Aaawk!* It was some kind of bird, but we didn't recognize the call. It grew louder. Even though I was very tired, I decided to climb the cliffs to try to find it.

Most birds in Greenland are visitors from afar. Birds like the Arctic tern and the snow bunting migrate from different areas to summer and nest on the coast. Only a few birds, including the raven and the snowy owl, spend the entire year in the Arctic.

I climbed and climbed. It wasn't until I was high enough to peer over the summit that I saw a large raven flying from rock to rock while holding something in its claws.

Called *tulugaq* (too-LOO-gake) in the Inuit language, the raven is believed to be a messenger, a creator, sometimes even a trickster. Ravens can communicate with all living things, but they rarely let humans come close. Why didn't the raven fly away from me as I climbed toward it? Instead, it flew closer.

The raven flew toward me; I climbed toward the raven. Soon, we were on the same rock. I had never been so close to a raven! We looked carefully at each other. The raven had a strong wedged beak, shiny feathers, and deep black eyes.

I could now see that it was not holding something but was badly tangled with musk ox fur and a stick. Perhaps this was a female raven and she had become snarled while building a nest. The tight tangle would surely damage her foot and prevent her from gathering food for her young ones.

I didn't want to scare her away, so I began speaking softly. I told her that I was sad, tired, and afraid. The harsh Arctic was too hard for me, and I didn't think I had the strength for the long journey ahead.

As I talked, the raven looked back at me. Then, with her sharp beak, she picked up a small rock, showed it to me, and set it back down. I picked up the rock and held it tightly.

I said no more words, but I thought about many things. I thought about vast Greenland and its animals and people. I thought of the graceful minke whales swimming in the sea during a storm. I remembered the small, beautiful wildflowers growing in the cold, rocky ground. I thought about all the preparation for the expedition and my friends and family who had helped in so many ways.

For the first time in a long time, I felt strong again.

I put the rock down and quickly scooped the raven into my arms. I began to unravel the musk ox fur from around her claw. It was badly knotted, and loosening the tangle took a long time.

Finally, her foot was free, and I threw the raven into the air. She flew in a circle and landed on a rock in front of me. Then she squawked and flew off over the cliff from where she had come.

Early the next morning, John and I started kayaking again. We traveled for four more stormy months and reached a small village called Kullorsuaq (koo-LORE-soo-ake). We had paddled 1,250 miles.

The rest of that winter and spring we traveled through northern Greenland by skis and dogsled. We endured many blizzards with temperatures reaching as low as –60 degrees Fahrenheit. The following summer, we kayaked south along the east coast and around to the southwest of Greenland. We paddled and pulled our kayak along the ice-packed shore, ending our journey in the village of Qaqortoq (KOE-ker-toke).

Every day I would look for ravens and remember the one who taught me that strength and spirit is in the land, in the sea, and in all living things. It is within us all, but we must search and find it for ourselves.

After fifteen months and 3,200 miles of travel, we finally finished the expedition. It was time to go home and see my family and friends at last. I couldn't wait to tell them all about Greenland and, of course, about the raven and her gift.